MARVEL STUD1OS

THE FIRST TEN YEARS

MARVEL STUD10S
THE FIRST TEN YEARS
READER COLLECTION

LITTLE, BROWN AND COMPANY
New York   Boston

Marvel's Guardians of the Galaxy: Friends and Foes originally published in July 2014 by Little, Brown and Company

Marvel's Ant-Man: I Am Ant-Man originally published in June 2015 by Little, Brown and Company

Marvel's Captain America: Civil War: We Are the Avengers originally published in April 2016 by Little, Brown and Company

Marvel's Thor: Ragnarok: Thor vs. Hulk originally published in October 2017 by Little, Brown and Company

Marvel's Black Panther: Meet Black Panther originally published in January 2018 by Little, Brown and Company

Cover design by Elaine Lopez-Levine.

Little, Brown and Company
Hachette Book Group
1290 Avenue of the Americas, New York, NY 10104
Visit us at LBYR.com

First Bindup Edition: October 2018

Little, Brown and Company is a division of Hachette Book Group, Inc. The Little, Brown name and logo are trademarks of Hachette Book Group, Inc.

The publisher is not responsible for websites (or their content) that are not owned by the publisher.

ISBN: 978-0-316-45310-3

Printed in the United States of America

CW

10 9 8 7 6 5 4 3 2

Passport to Reading titles are leveled by independent reviewers applying the standards developed by Irene Fountas and Gay Su Pinnell in *Matching Books to Readers: Using Leveled Books in Guided Reading*, Heinemann, 1999.

TABLE OF CONTENTS

GUARDIANS OF THE GALAXY
Friends and Foes 1

ANT-MAN
I Am Ant-Man.. 31

CAPTAIN AMERICA: CIVIL WAR
We Are the Avengers 61

THOR: RAGNAROK
Thor vs. Hulk.. 91

BLACK PANTHER
Meet Black Panther 121

MARVEL
GUARDIANS OF THE GALAXY

FRIENDS and FOES

By **Chris Strathearn**

Illustrated by Ron Lim, Drew Geraci, and Lee Duhig

Based on the Screenplay by James Gunn

Story by Nicole Perlman and James Gunn

Produced by Kevin Feige, p.g.a.

Directed by James Gunn

LITTLE, BROWN AND COMPANY
New York   Boston

Attention, GUARDIANS OF THE GALAXY fans! Look for these words when you read this book. Can you spot them all?

Orb

spaceship

tape player

soldiers

A magic Orb is hidden
on the planet of Morag.
It is an object of power.
It can be used for good—or evil.

Someone must protect the Orb
and keep the galaxy safe.
If it were used for evil,
the Orb could destroy everything.

Peter Quill finds the Orb.

He does not know about its power,

but he knows it can be sold.

Peter is from Terra.

This planet is also called Earth.

Peter is a space adventurer.

He is also called Star-Lord.

His spaceship is called the Milano.

But thanks to his ankle thrusters, he can fly without it!

His favorite thing is his tape player.

Peter grew up in space

with a group of aliens

called the Ravagers.

They find treasure and sell it.

Their motto is: "Steal from everybody!"

Yondu Udonta is the Ravager leader.
He has blue skin and red eyes.
Yondu finds out Peter has the Orb—
and Yondu wants it!

Peter needs friends to help him
keep the Orb safe.
Rocket Raccoon is his friend.
Rocket is a short alien
who looks like a raccoon.
He is small, but he is tough!

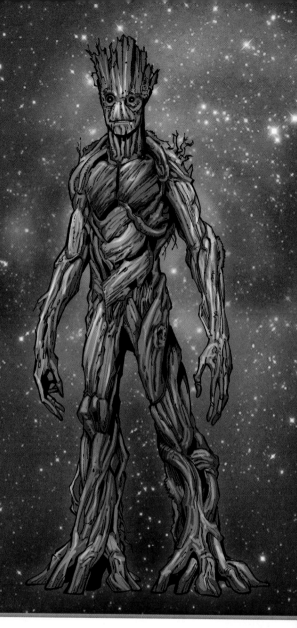

Rocket's best friend is Groot.
Groot is a big treelike being.
He can only say three words:
"I am Groot!"

Drax, another friend, is a skilled fighter.
His home world was destroyed,
and he does not like bad guys.
He is covered in tattoos.

Peter also asks for help from Gamora,
who is the last of her alien race.
Her skin is bright green.
Drax and Gamora agree to help Peter, too.

Thanos is a powerful being.

He always wins his battles.

He orders his people to bring him the Orb.

He wants to rule the galaxy.

If he gets the Orb, Thanos can use it to control planets. He must be stopped!

Ronan works for Thanos.

His Cosmi-Rod is a powerful weapon.

It makes everyone fear him.

Korath works for Ronan.

He is part robot and very strong.

He leads a group of soldiers

called Sakaarans.

Korath and his soldiers have spaceships
called Necrocraft.
They jet from planet to planet
looking for the Orb.
They will blast anyone in their way!

Nebula also works for Ronan.
She has blue skin and is part robot,
like Korath.
Nebula and Ronan set out
to find the Orb for Thanos.

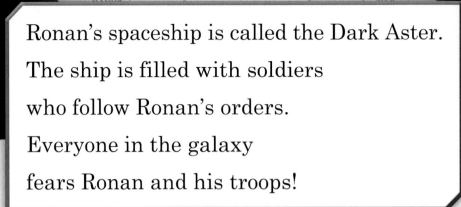

Ronan's spaceship is called the Dark Aster.
The ship is filled with soldiers
who follow Ronan's orders.
Everyone in the galaxy
fears Ronan and his troops!

The Nova Corps is a group
that polices the galaxy.
They try to stop Ronan
and other bad guys.

The Nova Corps protects aliens
and their home worlds.
They have been chasing
Ronan for a long time.

The Nova Corps fly in spaceships
called Starblasters.
The ships are fast.

Peter knows a lot of foes
are on their way to get the Orb.
Gamora says they should give the Orb
to the Collector.
The Collector will keep it safe.

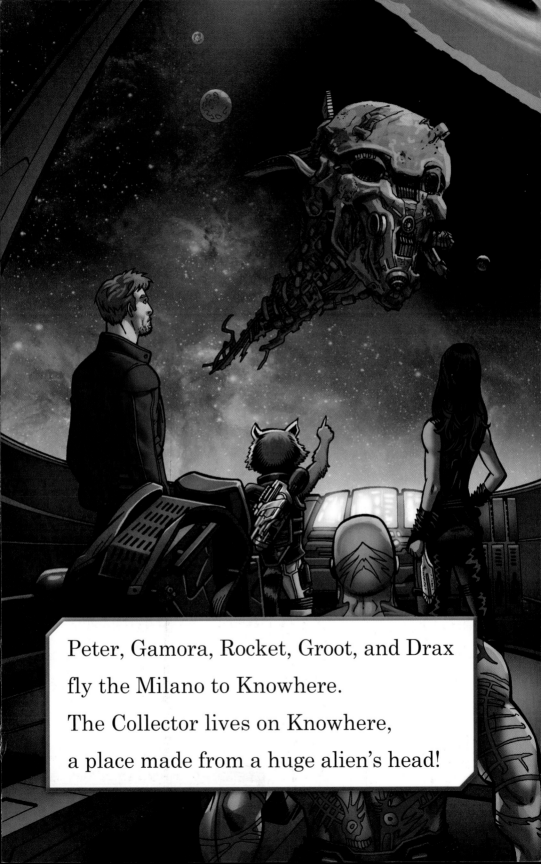

Peter, Gamora, Rocket, Groot, and Drax
fly the Milano to Knowhere.
The Collector lives on Knowhere,
a place made from a huge alien's head!

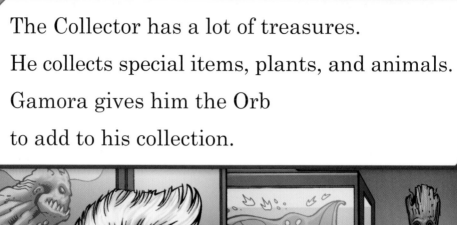

The Collector has a lot of treasures.

He collects special items, plants, and animals.

Gamora gives him the Orb

to add to his collection.

The Collector has a helper.

Her name is Carina.

When she takes the Orb from Gamora,

a powerful light flashes.

The Orb's power destroys

the Collector's home!

Just then, Ronan and his soldiers
appear on Knowhere!
If Ronan can get the Orb,
he will give it to Thanos!

Peter, Rocket, Groot, Drax, and Gamora will fight Ronan.

They are the Guardians of the Galaxy!

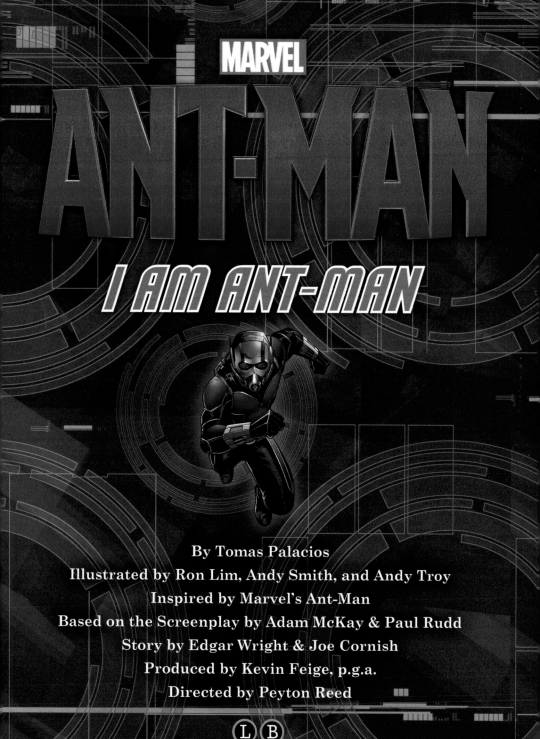

MARVEL

ANT-MAN

I AM ANT-MAN

By Tomas Palacios
Illustrated by Ron Lim, Andy Smith, and Andy Troy
Inspired by Marvel's Ant-Man
Based on the Screenplay by Adam McKay & Paul Rudd
Story by Edgar Wright & Joe Cornish
Produced by Kevin Feige, p.g.a.
Directed by Peyton Reed

(L)(B)
LITTLE, BROWN AND COMPANY
New York   Boston

Attention, Ant-Man fans!
Look for these words
when you read this book.
Can you spot them all?

suit

helmet

bathtub

match

Scott Lang did a bad thing.

He stole a lot of money.

Scott went away for a few years,
and now he wants to be good.

Scott has a daughter.

Her name is Cassie.

He does not get to see Cassie as much as he wants.

One day, Scott discovers a secret room. What is inside?

Scott takes the suit home and puts it on.
He looks really cool!

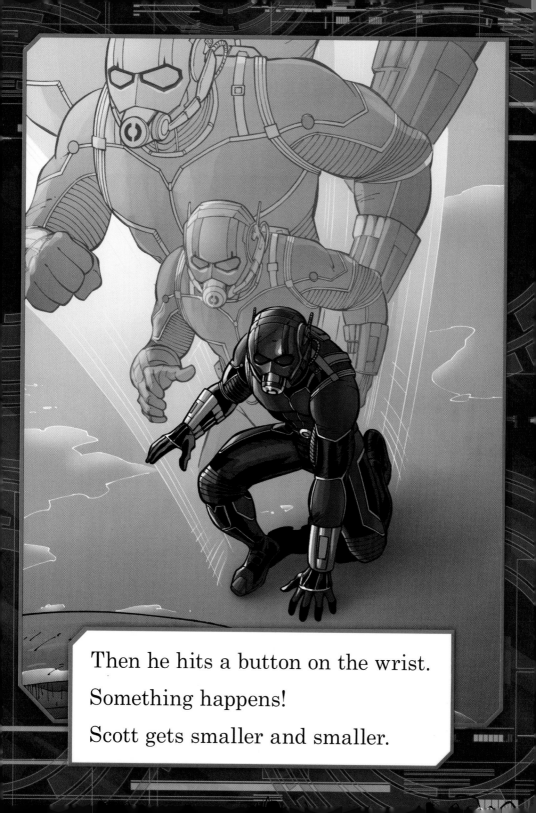

Then he hits a button on the wrist.

Something happens!

Scott gets smaller and smaller.

Scott is the size of an ant and is inside the bathtub! He sees a new world, and everything around him is bigger than before.

What is that sound?

Uh-oh!

Someone turned on the water.

It races toward Ant-Man like

a wild river!

Ant-Man runs as fast as he can.
Then he leaps into the air!
He makes it out of the tub and
falls through a crack in the floor.

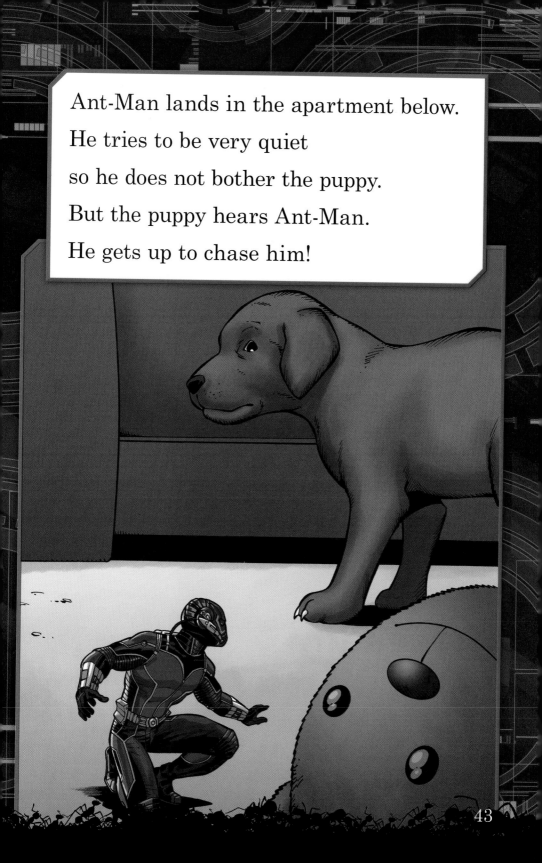

Ant-Man lands in the apartment below.

He tries to be very quiet

so he does not bother the puppy.

But the puppy hears Ant-Man.

He gets up to chase him!

Ant-Man learns he is faster when he is small.
He escapes the puppy and lands on something that spins and spins and spins! What is it?

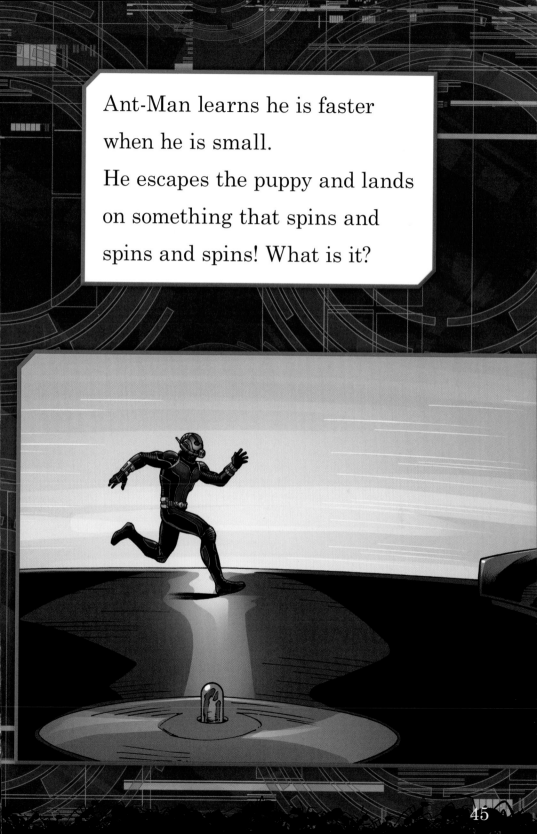

It is a record player!
Ant-Man is in the
middle of a party!
People dance all around him.
Ant-Man needs to be careful.
One stomp and he will be
flattened like a bug!

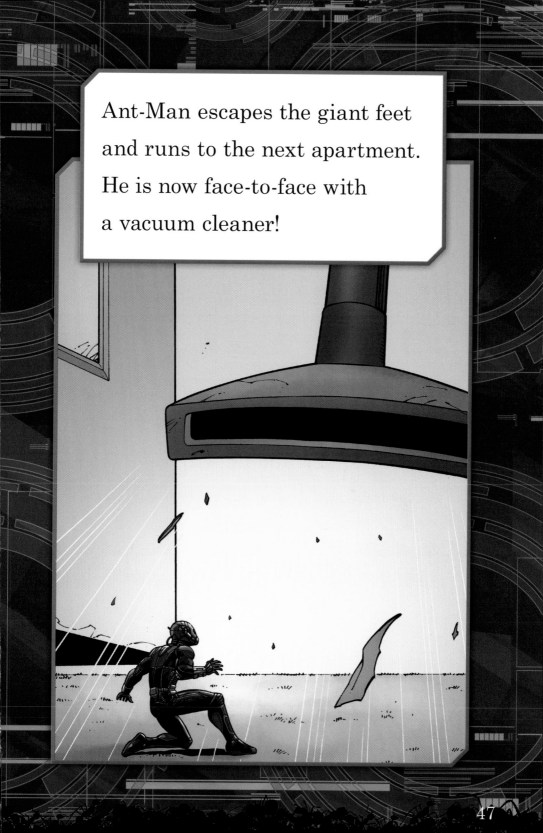

Ant-Man escapes the giant feet and runs to the next apartment. He is now face-to-face with a vacuum cleaner!

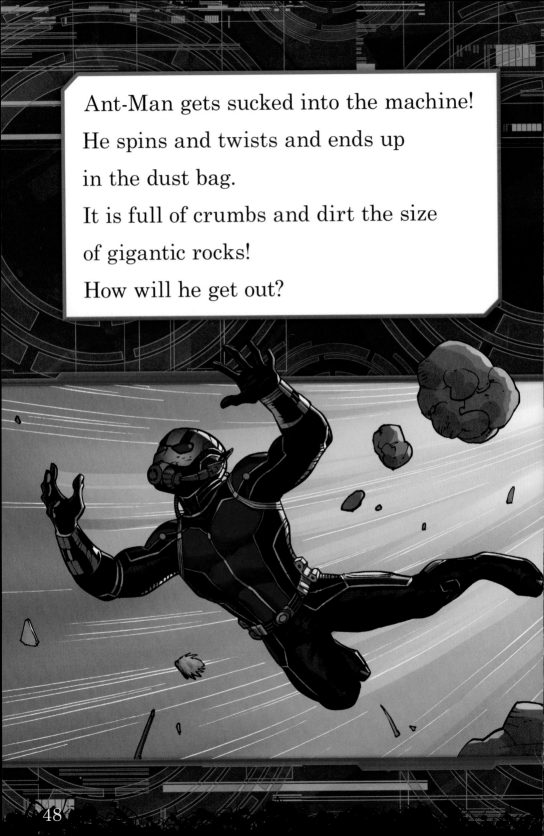

Ant-Man gets sucked into the machine!
He spins and twists and ends up
in the dust bag.
It is full of crumbs and dirt the size
of gigantic rocks!
How will he get out?

The woman vacuuming shakes the bag up and down. Ant-Man shoots out the side! He rockets across the room!

Ant-Man lands on a car
with a hard thump!
He dents the roof!
Ant-Man learns he is
tougher when he is small!

Ant-Man soon sees
a group of ants.
They circle around him.

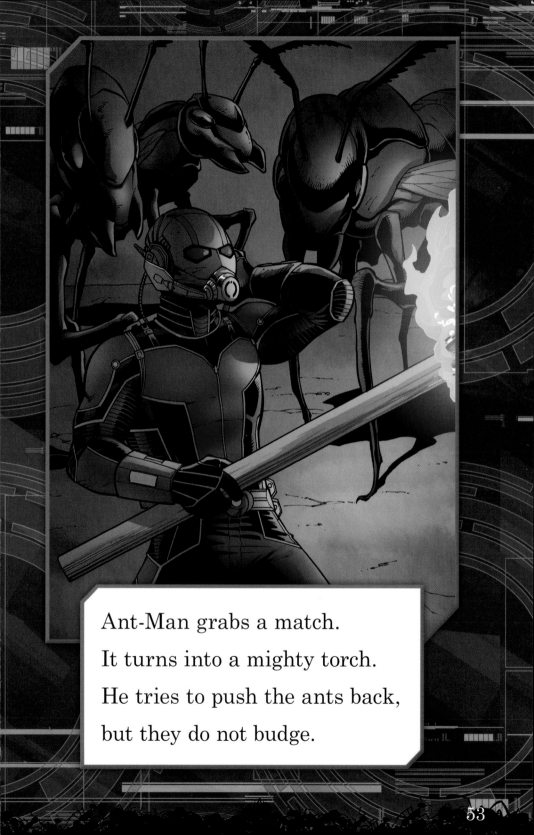

Ant-Man grabs a match.
It turns into a mighty torch.
He tries to push the ants back,
but they do not budge.

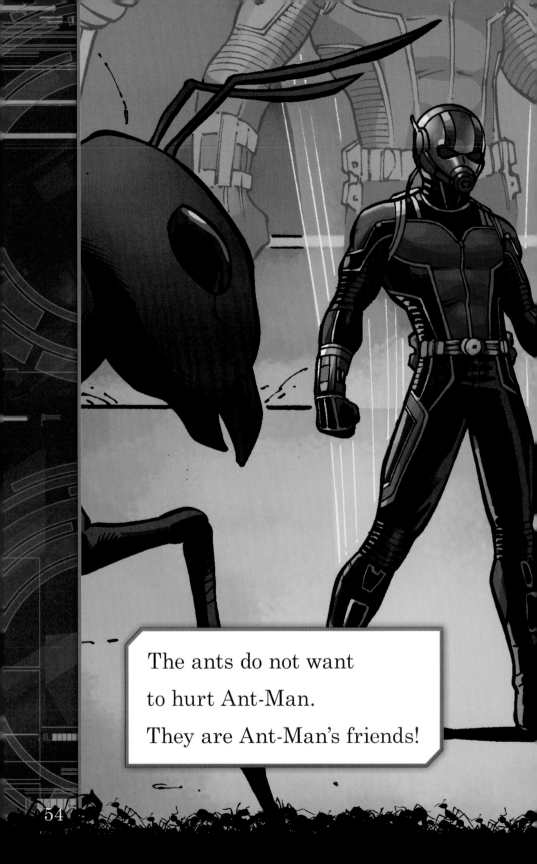

The ants do not want
to hurt Ant-Man.
They are Ant-Man's friends!

Ant-Man learns he has the power to talk to insects! They will do what he says!

Now Ant-Man has an army of ants!

Ant-Man climbs onto one.

His name is Ant-Thony.

He leads the charge!

The ants fly away!

Ant-Man protects Cassie from a bully.
Ant-Man does not like bullies.

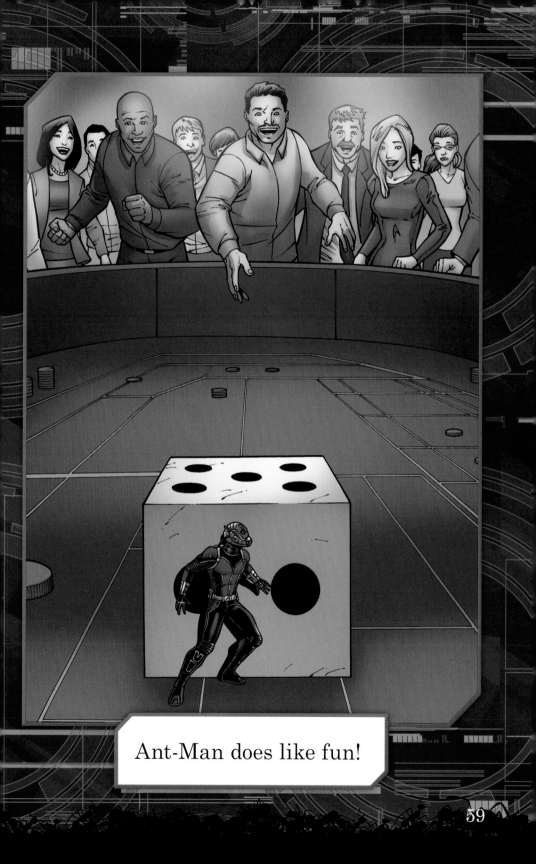

Ant-Man does like fun!

What Ant-Man likes most
is protecting Cassie.
Ant-Man feels good.
He is a real Super Hero!

MARVEL
CIVIL WAR
CAPTAIN AMERICA
WE ARE THE AVENGERS

Adapted by A. Harrison Smith

Illustrated by Ron Lim, Andy Smith, and Andy Troy

Based on the screenplay by Christopher Markus
& Stephen McFeely

Produced by Kevin Feige, p.g.a.

Directed by Anthony and Joe Russo

LITTLE, BROWN AND COMPANY
New York   Boston

Attention, Captain America fans!
Look for these words
when you read this book.
Can you spot them all?

shield

wings

mask

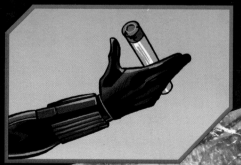

tube

The Avengers are Earth's Mightiest Heroes!
They fight in many battles.

They work together as a team,
and keep the world safe.

Steve Rogers is Captain America.

He is the leader of the Avengers.

His shield can stop almost anything.

Tony Stark is Iron Man.
His metal suit is very strong.
He can fly through the air.

Natasha Romanoff is the Black Widow.

She is a super-spy.

She can move fast and fight hard.

Steve, Tony, and Natasha go on many missions. Now the Avengers have some new team members!

Scarlet Witch can float in the air.
She can move things with her mind
and has special powers.

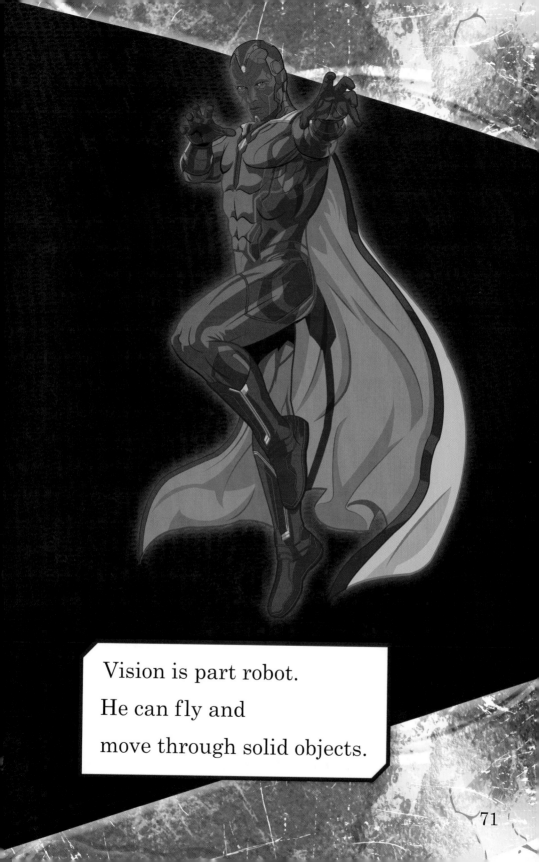

Vision is part robot.
He can fly and
move through solid objects.

War Machine has an iron suit.

He can fire missiles, just like Iron Man.

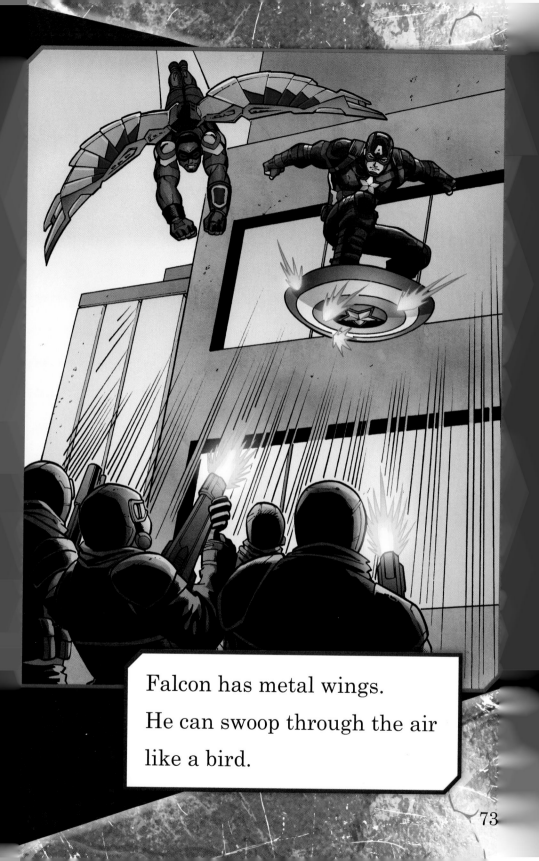

Falcon has metal wings.
He can swoop through the air
like a bird.

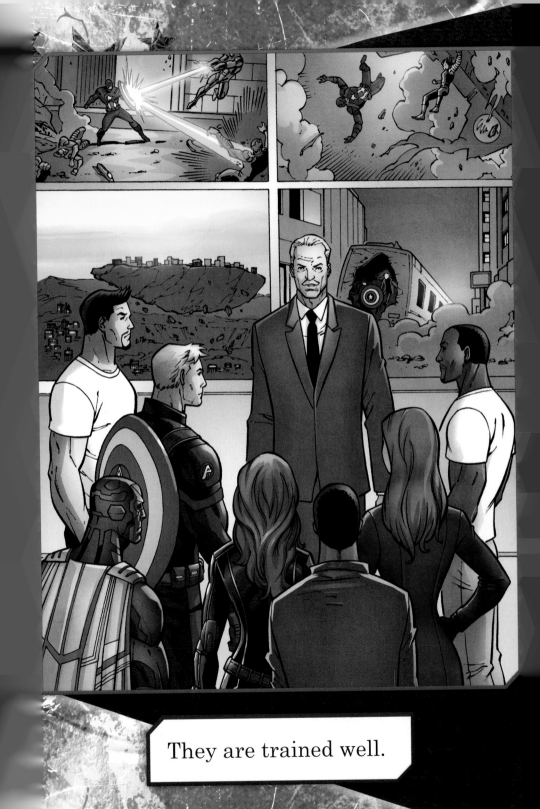

They are trained well.

Now the new team must save the day!

Crossbones was a S.H.I.E.L.D. agent.
He worked with Steve.

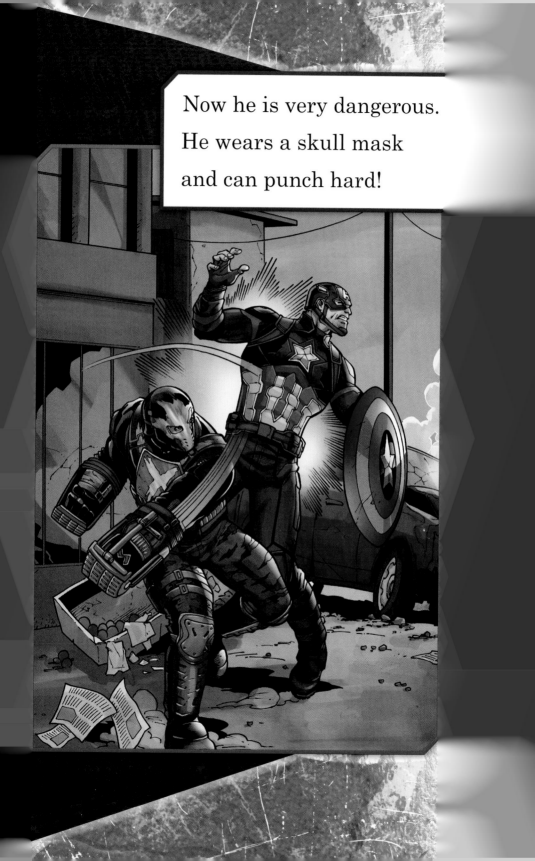

Now he is very dangerous.
He wears a skull mask
and can punch hard!

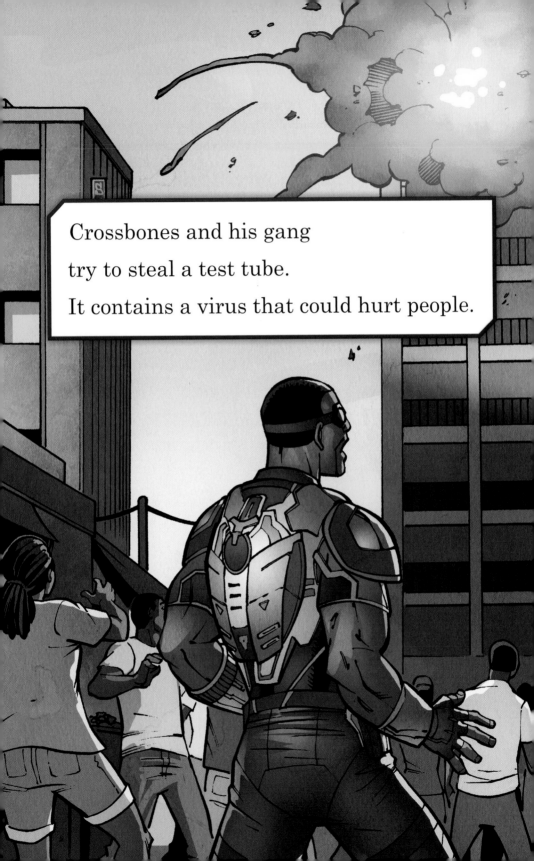

Crossbones and his gang
try to steal a test tube.
It contains a virus that could hurt people.

Captain America, Black Widow,
Scarlet Witch, and Falcon
must stop them.
But there is an explosion.
BOOM!

Crossbones leaps down
and attacks, but he is no match for Cap!

His team helps, too.

Black Widow finds the test tube.

Falcon joins the fight from above

SWOOSH!

There are always new battles to fight when you are an Avenger!

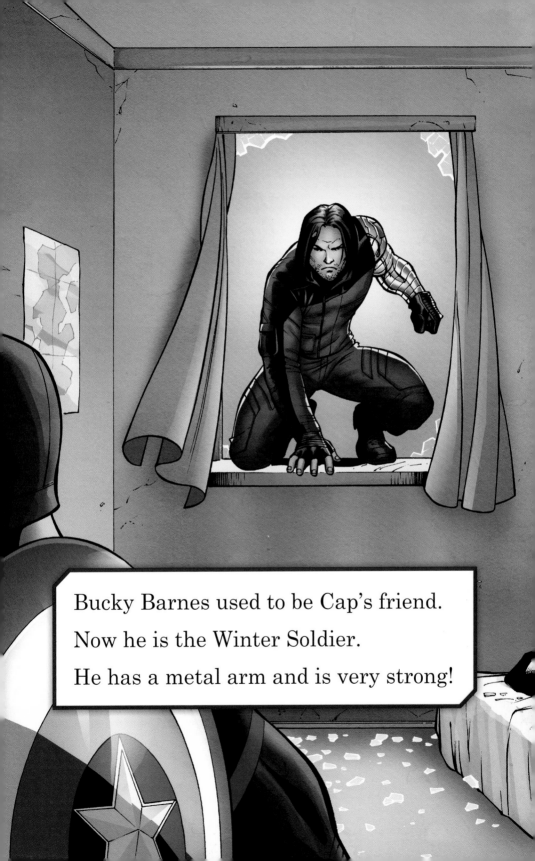

Bucky Barnes used to be Cap's friend.

Now he is the Winter Soldier.

He has a metal arm and is very strong!

Cap is looking for Bucky,
but he is not the only one.

Black Panther is also on the hunt.
He wears body armor
and a mask that has catlike ears.

Black Panther attacks Bucky.

They fight hard!

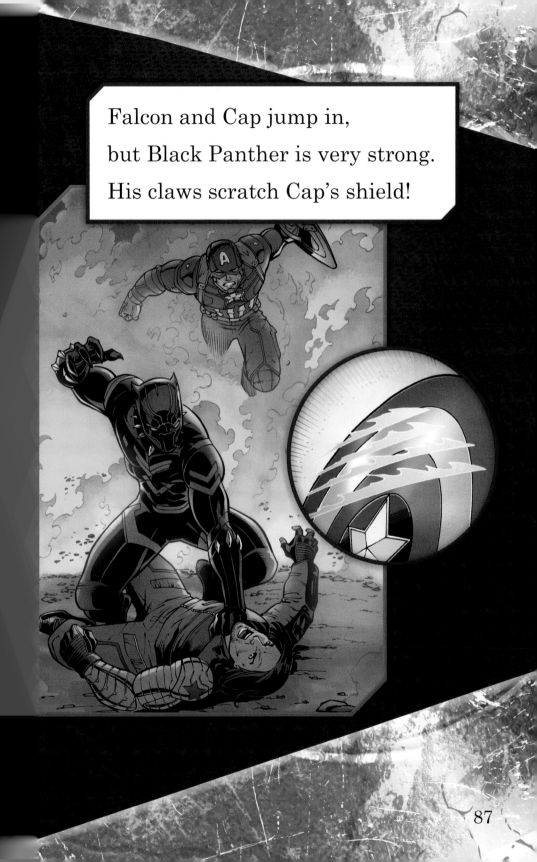

Falcon and Cap jump in,
but Black Panther is very strong.
His claws scratch Cap's shield!

War Machine arrives just in time!
He fires missiles.

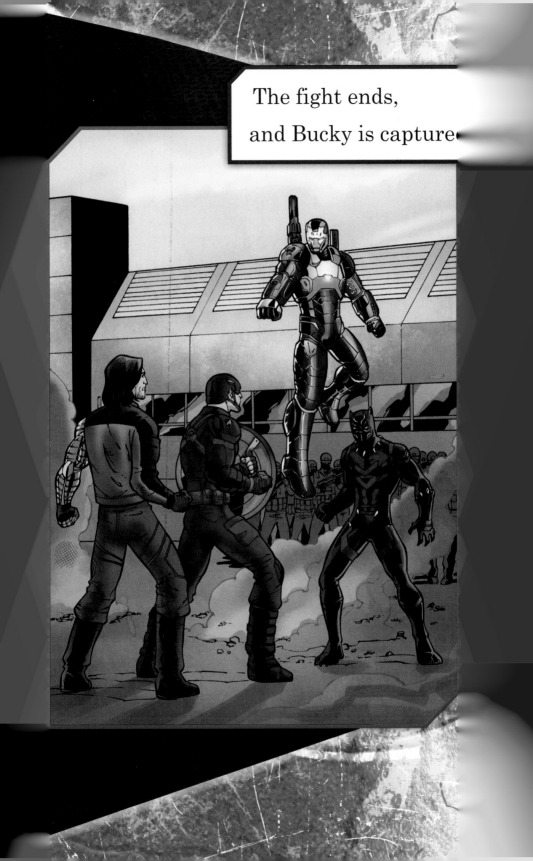

The fight ends,
and Bucky is captured.

MARVEL
THOR
RAGNAROK
THOR VS. HULK

Adapted by Justus Lee

Illustrations by Ron Lim

Written by Eric Pearson and

Craig Kyle & Christopher L. Yost

Produced by Kevin Feige, p.g.a.

Directed by Taika Waititi

LITTLE, BROWN AND COMPANY

New York   Boston

Attention, THOR fans!
Look for these words when you read
this book! Can you spot them all?

hammer

garbage

aliens

punch

This is Thor!
He has a magic hammer
called Mjolnir.

Thor returns to Asgard
after a big fight.
Thor thinks his father, Odin,
is acting strangely.

It is Loki disguised as Odin!
Thor is angry with his tricky brother.
Thor makes Loki tell him
where the real Odin is.

Thor and Loki find Odin on Earth.
When they return home by
using a bridge called the Bifrost,
something huge pushes Thor off it!

Thor wakes up on a very strange planet.

He is surrounded by garbage.

He is definitely not on Asgard.

A group of aliens surrounds Thor.
They shoot a net that shocks him
with electricity.
But a woman arrives and saves him.
Who is she?

Her name is Valkyrie.
She works for the ruler
of this planet.
She takes Thor to see
the Grandmaster.

He wants Thor to fight in his contest.
Thor is very good at fighting.
The Grandmaster says he will let
Thor leave if Thor wins.

A crowd is ready to watch the fight.
The Grandmaster says Thor
will battle the current Champion.
The people go wild!

Thor is prepared to fight anyone!
The current Champion
is the Hulk, Thor's friend
and a fellow Avenger!
They have not seen each other
in a long time.

Thor asks the Hulk for help escaping,
but the Hulk just wants to fight.
The Hulk runs toward Thor.

Thor does not want to,
but he has to fight.
They battle and the crowd cheers.

They fight as hard as they can.

They each have armor.

They each are very strong.

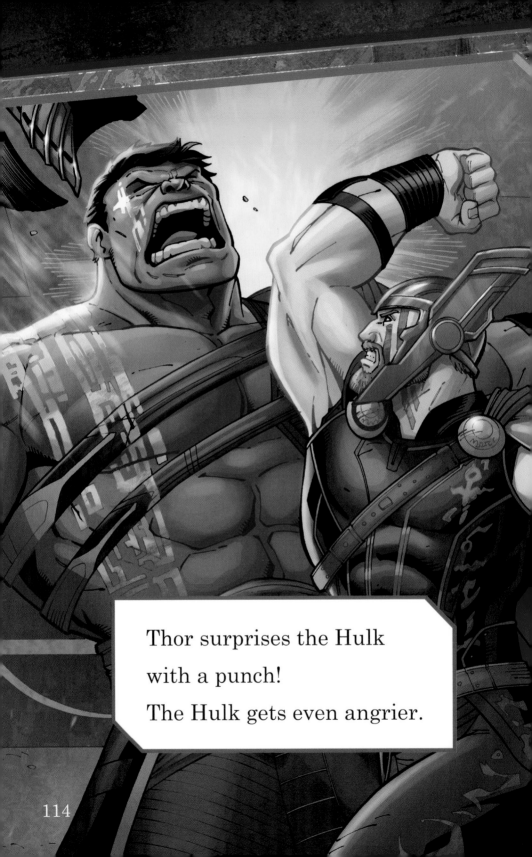

Thor surprises the Hulk
with a punch!
The Hulk gets even angrier.

The Hulk throws Thor against a wall.
Thor wants them to stop fighting
before they really hurt each other.

He takes Thor by the foot
and throws him against the floor.

Thor is very tired.

The Hulk jumps to smash his friend!

Thor wakes up later in a big room.
The Hulk now remembers that
Thor is his friend.
Valkyrie has decided to help them.
Thor needs to go home
to save Asgard!

MARVEL
BLACK PANTHER

MEET BLACK PANTHER

Adapted by R. R. Busse

Illustrations by Steve Kurth

Produced by Kevin Feige, p.g.a.

Directed by Ryan Coogler

Written by Ryan Coogler &
Joe Robert Cole

LITTLE, BROWN AND COMPANY
New York   Boston

121

Attention, BLACK PANTHER fans! Look for these words when you read this book. Can you spot them all?

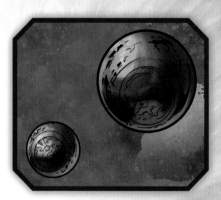

beads

fighter

doctor

chase

This is Black Panther!
He is also named T'Challa.
He is the next king of Wakanda.
He has a special suit and
is very smart.

Black Panther jumps into action
to help his people.
His sister, Shuri, invents beads
that help Black Panther.
Her inventions are very useful.

Black Panther's beads stop the trucks full of strangers. He waits in the shadows. He plans his next move.

T'Challa stops the bad guys!

His plans always work.

He is very fast.

Then he sees Nakia.

They were friends when they were kids.

She is on a mission for Wakanda, too.

T'Challa and Nakia played
together when T'Challa was
the prince of Wakanda.
Now Nakia helps people
around the world.
She is a great fighter, too.

133

T'Challa is happy to go back home.
He talks to his mother, Ramonda.
They remember his father.
T'Chaka was a great king.
He and Ramonda raised T'Challa
to do what is right.

While he is home in Wakanda, T'Challa talks to his sister, Shuri. Shuri is so smart! She makes all of Black Panther's gadgets.

She makes T'Challa a brand-new Black Panther suit. This suit absorbs attacks!

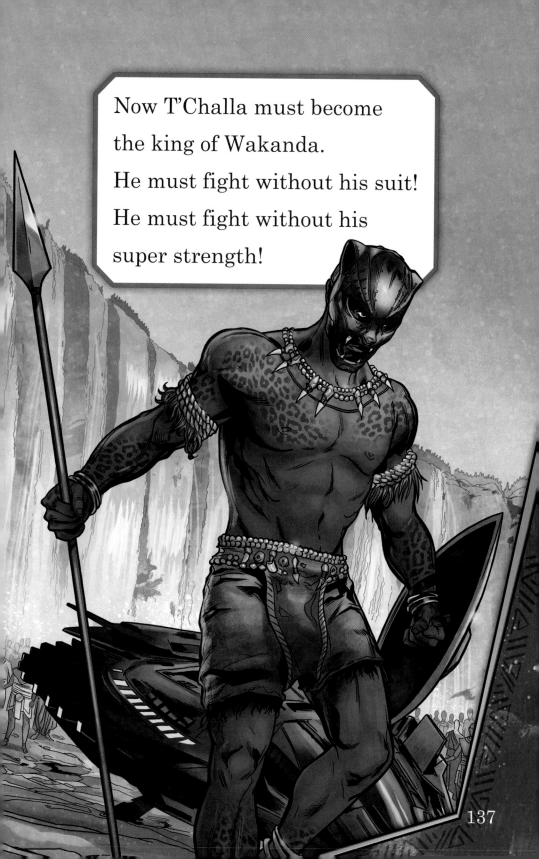

Now T'Challa must become the king of Wakanda. He must fight without his suit! He must fight without his super strength!

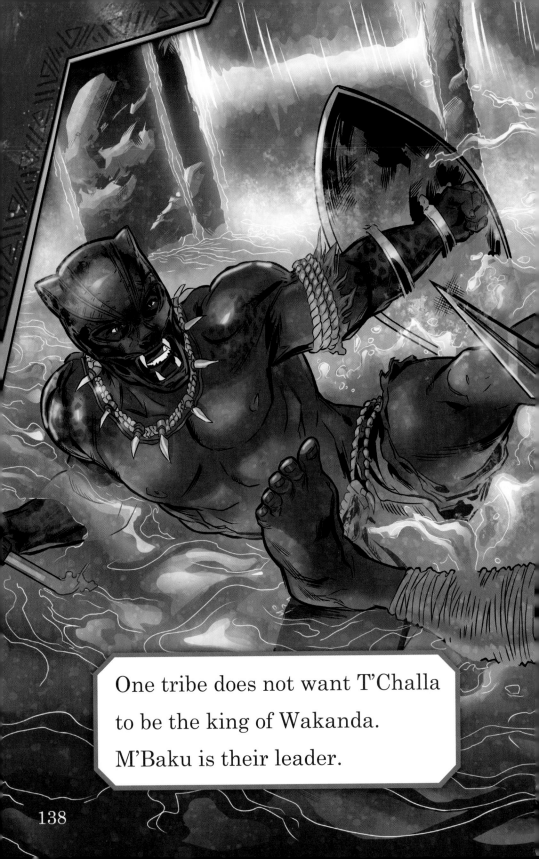

One tribe does not want T'Challa
to be the king of Wakanda.
M'Baku is their leader.

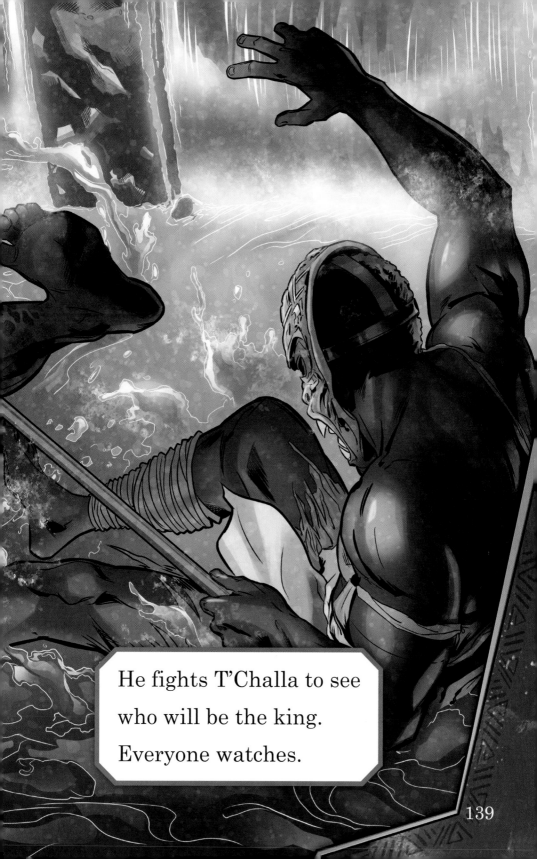

He fights T'Challa to see who will be the king. Everyone watches.

T'Challa must beat M'Baku. The fight is close, but T'Challa wins! He is a great fighter even without his suit.

After his fight, T'Challa needs to rest.
Zuri takes care of him.
He is the best doctor in the Golden City.
He restores T'Challa's strength and
talks about his father.

But Black Panther cannot rest for long.

Okoye has bad news.

She is a member of the royal guard.

She is one of the best warriors

in Wakanda, too.

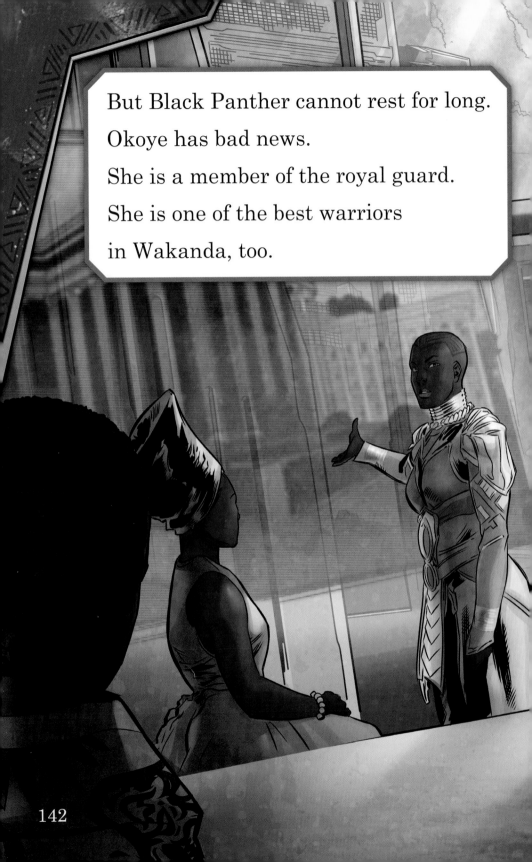

Ulysses Klaue stole something important!
It is Wakandan vibranium!
T'Challa must catch Klaue.

Erik Killmonger will do anything to help Klaue.

He wants money and power.

He helps Klaue try to sell the vibranium.

CIA agent Everett K. Ross

sets a trap!

He catches the villains.

Ross is friends with T'Challa.

Klaue and Killmonger try to escape the trap.

Luckily, Black Panther is close!

Black Panther will not let them get away.

The chase is on!
Can Black Panther catch
Klaue and save Wakanda?

CHECKPOINTS IN THIS BOOK ✔

Friends and Foes

WORD COUNT	GUIDED READING LEVEL	NUMBER OF DOLCH SIGHT WORDS
604	K	86

I Am Ant-Man

WORD COUNT	GUIDED READING LEVEL	NUMBER OF DOLCH SIGHT WORDS
486	K	68

We Are the Avengers

WORD COUNT	GUIDED READING LEVEL	NUMBER OF DOLCH SIGHT WORDS
388	K	67

Thor vs. Hulk

WORD COUNT	GUIDED READING LEVEL	NUMBER OF DOLCH SIGHT WORDS
373	K	64

Meet Black Panther

WORD COUNT	GUIDED READING LEVEL	NUMBER OF DOLCH SIGHT WORDS
403	K	70